MW00896375

Get set with Read Alone!

This entertaining series is designed for all new readers who want to start reading a whole book on their own.

The stories are lively and fun, with lots of illustrations and clear, large type, to make first solo reading a perfect pleasure!

Margaret Joy

Gertie's Gang

Illustrated by Toni Goffe

VIKING

VIKING

Published by the Penguin Group
27 Wrights Lane, London W8 5TZ, England
Viking Penguin Inc., 40 West 23rd Street, New York, New York 10010, USA
Penguin Books Australia Ltd, Ringwood, Victoria, Australia
Penguin Books Canada Ltd, 2801 John Street, Markham, Ontario, Canada L3R 1B4
Penguin Books (NZ) Ltd, 182–190 Wairau Road, Auckland 10, New Zealand

Penguin Books Ltd, Registered Offices: Harmondsworth, Middlesex, England

First published 1990

10 9 8 7 6 5 4 3 2 1

Text copyright © Margaret Joy, 1990
Illustrations copyright © Toni Goffe, 1990

The moral rights of the author has been asserted

All rights reserved. Without limiting the rights under copyright reserved above,
no part of this publication may be reproduced, stored in or introduced into a
retrieval system, or transmitted, in any form or by any means (electronic,
mechanical, photocopying, recording or otherwise), without the prior written
permission of both the copyright owner and the above publisher of this book

Filmset in Linotron Times by Rowland Phototypesetting (London) Ltd
Printed in Great Britain by Butler & Tanner Ltd, Frome and London

A CIP catalogue record for this book is available from the British Library

ISBN 0–670–83079–8

Contents

Gertie is Superwoman

It was playtime.

All the children in the mobile were putting on their coats. It was a bit of a struggle. There wasn't much room and they had to push and squeeze.

"Watch out, Midge," said Tim, "you're standing on my scarf."

"Where's my coat? Who's

hidden my coat?" asked Lenny.

Podge was crawling around the floor, looking for his lunchbox. "Ouch, my finger," he cried. "You trod on my finger, Tim Smith."

"Ooh, sorry, Podge. Here, have a chocolate finger instead."

"There's no room in here," said Gertie. "I can't breathe. I'm going outside to put my coat on."

She pushed past them all and clattered down the steps. Then she laid her coat on the ground with the outside underneath.

Midge, Lenny, Podge and

Tim came out and watched.
   "I'm going to be
Superwoman," she said.

She got hold of the collar of her coat and threw it back over her head. It fell round her shoulders like a cloak. Then she did up the top button at the front.

"There – see – I'm Superwoman!" she cried.

Gertie flew off round the playground, with her cloak flapping behind her.

The others thought this was a good idea too. They did the same thing with their coats.

Then they flew round the playground being Superwoman or Superman. It was a good game. Gertie and her gang

played it whenever they went
outside at breaktime.

Next day Gertie said to Midge,
"Let's play Superwoman
again."

"Later," said Midge, "I've
got something to show you
first."

They went to the far corner of
the playground and crouched

down, heads close together.
Midge brought something out
of her pocket.

"Look what I found," she
said.

She opened her hand. She
had an old red lipstick and a
little pot half full of blue
eyeshadow.

"They were in the bin in Mum's bedroom," said Midge.

"Can we put them on?" asked Gertie.

"After school," said Midge.

"No – now," said Gertie, "I dare you."

"All right," said Midge.

She rubbed the lipstick across her lips.

"And your cheeks," said Gertie, "I dare you."

Midge rubbed a big spot of red on to each cheek.

"Now the blue," said Gertie, "I dare you."

Midge put her finger in the blue eyeshadow and rubbed it

all round her eyes.

Gertie looked at her.

"Great," she said, "make-up – just like Superwoman."

Midge put her Superwoman cloak on again.

Suddenly they heard shouting coming from the other side of the playground.

"There's that spotty dog," said Gertie. "It's got into the playground again."

"It's a big dog," said Midge.

"Yes, it makes some people scream," said Gertie.

"It has big teeth," said Midge.

"I know, I've seen them,"

said Gertie.

"It scares me stiff," said
Midge.

"It wouldn't scare
Superwoman," said Gertie.
"She'd go up to it and send it
packing."

"Would she?" asked Midge.

"Yes," said Gertie. "Go on. I dare you."

Midge started to run across the playground, her cloak flapping behind her. She ran faster and faster towards the big spotty dog, shouting, "Go away, go away, nasty spotty dog. Get out of here!"

The dog looked up and saw something coming towards him. It was running and flapping, and its face was all red and blue, and it was shouting very loudly. The spotty dog was scared stiff. He ran out of the school gate as fast as he could.

Midge and Gertie stood on the gate and poked their heads over it. They watched the dog galloping away up the road.

"Great," said Gertie, "you were just like Superwoman. Now go and show Mrs Parry your face – I dare you."

Fetching the Bell

One day Mrs Parry was on playground duty. She was walking round, keeping an eye on all the children.

Some were playing leap-frog; some were doing handstands; some were looking at football cards; some were chasing one another; others were just standing together and chatting.

Midge and Gertie came running up to Mrs Parry.

"Careful now," she said, "this coffee's very hot. I don't want it to spill on you."

"Can we take the mug back
to the staff-room for you?"
asked Gertie.

"When you've finished," said
Midge.
"Yes, just let me drink the

last few mouthfuls," said Mrs Parry.

They walked round with her for a few more minutes until she had finished her coffee. Then she said:

"You can carry the mug, Gertie, and you can knock on the staff-room door, Midge. And when you're there, ask if you can have the bell, and then bring it back to me. But first you can each have half of my biscuit."

They popped the half-biscuit in their mouths and set off across the playground, munching.

When they reached the staff-room, Miss Green opened the door. She took the mug. Then Gertie said, "Please could we take the bell to Mrs Parry?"

"The bell? The bell?" said Miss Green, looking round. "I can't see it at the moment. I'll have to look for it. Perhaps you could go and fetch the radio for me while I search for the bell. Will you do that?"

The two girls nodded and went along to the hall. They found the radio. It was large and heavy, with sharp corners that bumped against their legs. They had to keep stopping to

take turns carrying it. At last
they reached the staff-room.

"Phew," said Midge, "this
weighs a ton, and I'm out of
breath."

"Me too!" puffed Gertie.

They knocked on the door.

"Oh, thank you very much," said Miss Green. "I've not had much luck finding the bell, I'm afraid. It doesn't seem to be here. I think someone must have left it on the shelf next to the side door. Could you go and have a look?"

Gertie and Midge nodded and began to make their way there when Mr Roberts came rushing up.

"Ah," he said, "a couple of sensible girls. Just the people I need. Could you go to the kitchen and ask Cook for a plastic bin bag? There's litter

blowing all over the
playground. I want it picked up
as soon as possible."

"But –"

"But –" said Midge and
Gertie together.

"Off you go now," said Mr Roberts.

He didn't give them time to explain about the bell, so they went to the kitchen and asked Cook for a plastic bin bag.

"Of course," she said, "here you are. But on your way back could you put these cabbage leaves in your classroom? They're left over, and they'll do for Wuffles. Go on now," she said, "there's just time before the bell rings."

"But –"

"But –"

She didn't give Midge and Gertie time to explain about the

bell, so they hurried to their
classroom and left the cabbage
leaves next to the rabbit hutch.
(But first they opened the door
of the hutch and pushed in a
leaf for Wuffles for his lunch.)

Next they took the bin bag to
the staff-room and gave it to Mr

Roberts. Then they hurried off to the side door to get the bell.

"I can see it on the shelf," said Midge.

"Thank goodness – at last!" said Gertie.

She lifted it down by its wooden handle. She held the clapper of the bell with her other hand, so that it wouldn't make a noise. Then the two girls went out into the playground and ran across to Mrs Parry.

"Where *have* you been?" she asked.

"We had to help Miss Green."

"And Mr Roberts."

"And Cook."

"And Wuffles."

"And me," added Mrs Parry, smiling. "Thank you very much, both of you – and now you can each take a turn at ringing the bell."

"Great," said Gertie, and she let go of the clapper.

She swung the bell to and fro.

Ding-a-ling-a-ling-a-ling.

"Now my go," said Midge. She took the bell from her friend. She began to shout.

"It's the end of playtime, everybody!"

Ding-a-ling-a-ling-a-ling!

No Plasters for Gertie

One dinner-time, Gertie and her gang were playing leap-frog. Tim, Lenny, Podge and Midge bent over. Gertie ran towards Tim, put her hands flat on his back and jumped over him.

Then she did the same with Lenny, Podge and Midge.

"Jumped you all!" she said.

Tim stood up straight. "My turn now," he said.

He jumped over Lenny, Podge, Midge and Gertie.

Then it was Lenny's turn.

He ran and put his hands flat on Midge's back. But her back was wobbly, and Lenny was heavy. He didn't jump high enough and he fell on top of Midge.

"Ow-ee!" she said. "Watch out!"

"Ow-ow-ow!" cried Lenny. "My elbow!"

He twisted his arm round to look at his elbow.

"Blood!" he cried. "I'm

bleeding. Ow-ow-ow!"

He ran off into school. The others went on playing. When Lenny came out again, he had stopped crying.

"Look at my plaster," he said proudly.

He showed them all the big plaster on his elbow.

"Huh," said Gertie, "what a fuss about a little bit of blood. Anyway, I've had enough of leap-frog. Let's play skipping."

She fetched her skipping-rope.

Tim and Podge turned the rope while Lenny just watched (because of his elbow). Midge and Gertie got ready to jump in.

"All in together now,
Never mind the weather now,
When it's your birthday,
Please jump in –
January, February, March, April–"

"MAY!" shouted Midge and Gertie together.

They both jumped in and
crashed into one another.
Gertie kept her balance, but
Midge went sprawling on to her
tummy and hands.

"Ow-ow-ow, my hands!" she
yelled.

She looked at her hands. One of them was grazed.

"Blood!" she yelled. "I'm bleeding. Ow-ow-ow!"

She got up and ran off into school.

When she came back, she had stopped yelling.

"Look at my hand," she said. "I've got a plaster too."

"Huh," said Gertie, "what a fuss about a little bit of blood. Anyway, I've had enough of skipping. I'm going on to the field to play football."

She wrapped her skipping-rope round her waist and ran off. Podge went with her. Some of the others in their class were already playing there.

"You can go in goal, Podge," they said.

It was a good game and they all got covered in mud. Then Podge dived to save a goal. The ball whizzed past him. He skidded in the mud and fell on his knees.

"Ow-ow-ow!" he howled. "I fell on a stone!"

He looked at his knees. "Blood!" he howled. "Blood and mud!"

He struggled to his feet and limped off into school. When he came back, his knees were pink again and he had a plaster on each of them.

"Look," he said, "*two* plasters!"

"Huh," said Gertie, "what a fuss about a little bit of blood."

She stomped away, back to the playground.

"You're in a bad temper," said Midge.

"Oh no I'm not," said Gertie.

"Yes you are, Gertie Lee – just because you haven't got a plaster on your hand like me."

"No I'm not," said Gertie.

"Yes you are," said Lenny.

"No I'm not," said Gertie.

"Yes you are," said Podge. "You want a plaster too."

"NO I DO NOT!" yelled Gertie.

She ran to thump them all, but she tripped and fell and bumped her forehead on the ground.

"Ow-ow-ow!" she screamed.

She felt her forehead and looked at her fingers.

"Blood!" she screamed.
"Help, help!"

Midge was kind-hearted. She
put her arm round her friend
and helped her into school.

Mrs Parry phoned for
Gertie's mother to come. Her
mother took her to the doctor's.
The doctor had to stitch Gertie's
cut. She had three stitches
altogether.

She came back to school the next day, looking rather pale.

"The doctor said I could have a plaster or stitches," she said, "so I chose stitches. Lots of people have plasters, but I think stitches are more *interesting*."

The Seagull-with-one-leg

Gertie and her friends were in the playground. They were playing marbles.

"Now it's my shot," said Podge.

He aimed at Tim's green marble. Click.

"Got it!" he shouted. He waved his arms in the air.

But the others weren't

listening. They were looking towards the school field. Lots of birds were flying around overhead. They began to come down and land. They flapped their big grey and white wings, then settled on the grass.

"The seagulls have landed," said Gertie.

"That means it's going to rain," said Midge. "The seagulls always come down on our field when rain's coming."

"Hey – look over there," Tim shouted. "That seagull's standing on one leg."

"Oh yes," said Midge.

"It's only got one leg!" cried Lenny.

"It must have had an accident," said Podge.

"Perhaps it was run over."

"Or got into a fight with a cat."

"Or got too close to a shark in the sea."

"It's very good at balancing," said Gertie.

They watched the Seagull-with-one-leg until the bell rang and they had to go in.

It was time for PE. They took off their shoes and socks and went into the hall.

"We'd better put the lights on," said Mrs Parry. "It's getting quite dark."

"It's the clouds," said Lenny. "It's going to rain soon."

"Yes, the seagulls have

landed," said Gertie.

"We saw one with only one leg," said Midge.

They all went to look out of the window. The Seagull-with-one-leg was still there.

"He's very good at balancing," said Mrs Parry. "I wonder if you could all stand still on one leg like that."

They tried. It was very difficult. They swayed to and

fro. They wibbled and wobbled. Some of them had to put their other foot down. One or two others fell over.

"Now, can you hop on one leg like he does?" asked Mrs Parry.

That was easier. Most of them could hop on one leg.

"I have to hold my arms out to balance with," said Tim.

"Like wings," said Midge.

They hopped round the hall, holding out their wings.

"Now try with only one wing," said Mrs Parry.

That was really difficult. Everyone began to sway to and fro, then wibble and wobble. In the end they all fell over and laughed and laughed.

Gertie looked out of the window again. "They're flying away," she said.

"And the Seagull-with-one-leg is flying away too," said Lenny.

"Perhaps he'll come back another time," said Midge. "We'll have to look out for him."

Suddenly they heard a noise on the roof of the hall:

pitter-patter-pitter-patter-
pitter-patter . . .

"Here comes the rain," said
Mrs Parry.

"The seagulls were right,"
said Gertie.

"They're as good as the
weathermen on telly," said
Midge. "I wonder how they
know, when nobody's told
them . . ."

Scary Story-time

Nearly every day some of the children in Mrs Parry's class brought things to show her and their friends.

One day Lenny brought in his favourite book, full of fairy stories.

Podge brought in his new white football. It was a present from his uncle, who had won it

in a raffle.

At playtime everyone
crowded round to look at the
football.

"It's covered in writing," said
Midge.

"Those are the names of the
United team," said Podge.
"They've all signed it."

Everyone looked at the

writing – yes, there were lots of different names.

"It's a shame to play with it," said Tim. "It'll get dirty."

"It doesn't matter," said Podge. "Let's have a game now – I'll be captain."

They had a really exciting game of football. The whole class joined in. They all wanted to give the new ball a good kick.

Thud – thump – thud.

The ball was kicked up and down the school field. Now it was beginning to look like a real football, covered in mud and grass stains.

They played football again at dinner-time. Then they played again in the middle of the afternoon until the bell went.

"Ah no," said everyone. They didn't want to go in.

But then Lenny said, "It's story-time, and we're going to have a story out of my book."

So then they forgot the

football and ran back to the mobile. Their footsteps echoed as they thudded up the wooden steps and into the classroom. They were hot and red in the face, puffing and panting.

"I'm boiling," gasped Tim. He fanned himself with his hand.

"So am I," said Midge. "That was the best game yet."

"Phew," said the others. They wiped their faces with their arms and flapped their shirts to try to cool down.

"It's half past two," said Mrs Parry. "Story-time. Now try to sit still and you'll soon cool down."

She opened Lenny's book.

"Let's have a scary one," said
Tim.

"Well, I don't think any of
these are scary," said Mrs
Parry. "You know some of them
already. You know Little Red
Riding Hood, and you know

about Goldilocks and the Three Bears. You've heard the story of Jack and the Beanstalk, and the Elves and the Shoemaker, and Snow White and the Seven Dwarfs, and you know the story of the Gingerbread Man. How about the Wolf and the Seven Little Kids?"

"Yes, great – that sounds a bit scary," said everyone, and they settled down to listen.

"Once upon a time," began Mrs Parry, "there was a mother goat, who had seven little kids. They lived together in a little house and they were very happy. But a wolf lived near by, and they were all afraid of him. The mother goat used to tell her kids:

'Never let the wolf into the house – he might eat you.'

One day she had to go to town. But before she went, she said to her kids:

'If anyone knocks at the door,

don't let them in – it might be
the wolf –'"

Bang-bang-bang.

There was a loud knocking
noise. The mobile shook. The
children looked at one another
with wide eyes. Tim turned
pale.

"I'll go," said Gertie.

She tried to be brave. She opened the door and looked out.

"No one there!" gasped everyone. "Ooo-ooghh!"

"That's odd," said Mrs Parry. "Never mind, let's get on with the story." She went on:

"So the little kids promised. They said, 'We won't let anyone in – it might be the wolf –'"

Bang-bang-bang. The mobile shook again.

"Eeek," squealed Midge. "The wolf!"

"Nonsense," said Mrs Parry.

She got up and opened the door wide.

"No one there!" gasped everyone again. "Ooo-eeegh!"

They moved closer to one another and looked at Mrs Parry.

"That's very odd indeed," she said. "Never mind, let's get on with the story."

She went on:

"The mother goat went to

town and left the seven kids on their own. They began to play. Suddenly there was a loud knocking –"

Bang-bang-bang! The mobile shook again.

"Good heavens," said Mrs Parry, "this is past a joke."

This time she went right outside and down the steps. The children followed her; they didn't want to be left alone. They followed her round the side of the mobile.

Bang-bang-bang! The mobile echoed and shook.

"There it is again," said everyone.

They held their breath and
waited. Then they heard a tiny
voice.

"He-e-elp . . . Mrs Parry . . .
I'm stuck . . . he-e-elp . . ."

"It's coming from

underneath!" said Tim.

They all crouched down and looked under the mobile.

"It's Podge," they shouted. "He's stuck!"

Poor Podge was lying on his tummy under the mobile, wedged between some big stones. He couldn't move at all – except for one leg.

Bang-bang-bang. He kicked the bottom of the mobile with his leg. "He-e-elp . . ." he called again.

"We'll get you out," said Gertie.

She crawled underneath and took hold of his ankles. Then Midge crawled underneath and took hold of Gertie's ankles. Now Midge's ankles were sticking out, so Mrs Parry took hold of them and started to pull.

Slowly, slowly, Midge was pulled out, then Gertie, then Podge. He was covered in dust and looked a bit upset. But he had his arms round his precious football.

"It rolled under there after the bell went," he said, "and I crawled in to get it. Then I couldn't move. I thought I'd bang the floor, so you'd hear me."

"We did hear you," said everyone. "But we thought you were the wolf!"

Then they told Podge what had happened.

"It was the best story-time we've had for ages," said Tim. "Real scary."

A Day Out for Wuffles

It was a warm sunny day.

Everyone was in class in the mobile. It was very quiet. Mrs Parry was marking the register.

Crunch-crunch-crunch.

"What was that noise?" asked Podge.

"It's Wuffles," said Tim. "He's biting the wire on his cage."

"It's rabbit-talk," said Gertie. "He's telling us something."

Crunch-crunch-crunch.

"Perhaps he's telling us he wants to be outside," said Mrs Parry. "Why don't you take him out into the sunshine."

Gertie, Midge and Tim took hold of the hutch and carried it down the steps and out on to the grass. Lenny and Podge carried the run and put it down next to the hutch. They opened the hutch door.

"Come on, Wuffles – come and have a run," called Midge.

"He doesn't run, he hops," said Gertie.

Wuffles wuffled his nose and twitched his whiskers. Then he hopped out on to the grass. His black and white fur shone in the sun.

"Now let's take the tables and chairs outside and we can work in the sunshine," said Mrs Parry.

"Can we take the doll's house too?"

"And the cot and cradle?"

"And the building bricks?"

"Yes, yes, yes," said Mrs Parry. "There's plenty of room outside."

Everybody took something. Gertie and Midge carried the

trays of cress they had been growing.

"That's a good idea," said Mrs Parry. "You can water the cress out here."

After they had watered the cress, Midge and Gertie fetched their reading books. They sat in the sunshine and read stories to one another. Everybody else

was busy too. No one was
watching Wuffles . . .

When it was playtime they went
to buy some crisps. Then they
came back outside.

"Do rabbits like crisps?"
asked Gertie.

"Perhaps they do if they're
grass-flavoured," said Midge.

"Let's see if Wuffles likes crisps," said Gertie.

"He's not in his run," said Podge.

"He's not in his hutch either," said Lenny.

"He must have hopped out," said Tim. "Where's he gone?"

"There's a footprint here in the dirt," said Podge. "It's got claw-marks."

"Let's track him. Let's follow the footprints," said Lenny.

"There's another one here," said Gertie.

"And another one here," said Tim.

"And there are some rabbit

droppings here," said Podge. "We're on the right track."

"We're heading for the flower-bed," said Tim.

"There aren't any flowers in this bed," said Lenny. "They've all had their tops bitten off."

"Wuffles did it!" they all cried.

The tracks led from the soil of the flower-bed, along the flagstones and back to outside the classroom.

"Oh," cried Midge. "Look at our cress!"

"There isn't any left," said Gertie. "All the green tops have been nibbled off."

"Wuffles did it!" said
everyone.

"But where is he?" asked
Podge.

"There are no more tracks,"
said Lenny.

"He's not under the tables,"
said Midge.

"He's not in the doll's house,"
said Tim.

"But look who's lying in the cradle," said Gertie.

They crowded round to look. Wuffles was lying fast asleep on the blankets in the cradle. A few stalks of cress were sticking out of the corner of his mouth. He looked very fat – and very happy!

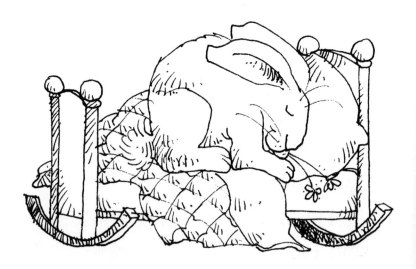